Written by Aleix

The Virtue of Patience

LOYOLA PRESS.

Why is it necessary to teach patience?

Patience is the important work we do while we are waiting for something to happen. Without patience, we can miss out on enjoying the rhythm of daily life, achieving our dreams, or fully developing our talents. Children who are guided in the practice of patience have a strong foundation on which to develop the self-regulatory behaviors that set the stage for happiness and success while lessening anxiety and frustration.

Although it may seem like some of us are born with more patience than others, all of us have to practice and grow in our capacity to exercise patience in situations big and small.

Children's concept of time differs greatly from that of adults, which can make developing the virtue of patience challenging but worth the effort. There is no doubt that to teach patience, you must have a great deal of it

yourself. Teaching about patience is best begun at an early age and should be taught as an active exercise in self-control. Highlight the joy of anticipation and satisfaction that children will feel when they have achieved a goal, acquired a new skill, made a new friend, or saw progress toward realizing a dream. Be patient with yourself and those you teach as you practice and apply this fundamental virtue.

The changing landscape

"Are we there yet? Is it far?" I ask my parents all the time when we drive in the car. Then they tell me that yes, we still have a way to go. Mom adds, "We have all this time to enjoy the landscape. Look out the window and watch it pass by. It's like we are at the movies. If we got there right away, we would not see the streams, the forests, the buildings, or the people."

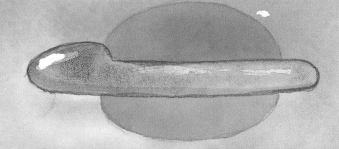

Goodbye, training wheels

When I was little, I rode a tricycle, but I wanted a bicycle like the older kids. "Patience," my cousin told me. "It takes time to learn how to keep your balance," continued my aunt. "Wait until your legs grow long enough to reach the pedals," added my uncle. Soon I could reach the pedals of my bicycle, but I needed some training wheels on each side so I wouldn't fall. Today, the training wheels were finally taken off. I'm grown up now!

On my own!

This morning, I opened the drawers and the closet. I took out a T-shirt, a sweater, and some pants. It took me a while to choose them. It was also a bit hard to put my clothes on. My parents do it quicker. But when I finished, I felt very proud that I had gotten dressed all by myself!

Book or movie?

We're reading a story at school. As we read, it seems like it will never end. "Why don't we just watch the movie?" we ask the teacher. "If we did that, we wouldn't have the pleasure of reading the story, would we?" she replies and adds, "Then you couldn't construct worlds and characters with your imagination."

Mixing Colors

"I've finished already! I'm the first to finish the drawing!" I exclaimed. "You've finished, but you'll have to start again. You haven't let the layers of paint dry. Now all the colors have mixed together," the teacher points out. "Do you see what happens when you go too fast?"

Nine months!

This morning, I met my sister. She took nine months to arrive. Nine! "That's a long time. I don't want to wait that long," I complained the day that they told me she was on her way. But during those nine months, we were able to carefully set up her new bedroom, choose her toys, and best of all, watch Mom's belly growing bigger and feeling the baby moving inside.

Taking turns

"Not all at the same time!" shout the older children. "Don't you know that you can't all play at the same time?" asks one of the parents. "You're not playing that game correctly," explains a grandmother. Then our teacher helps us understand, "While four of you play foosball, the others can watch how they play, learn what they do well, what mistakes they make, and think about how you will score a goal when it's your turn!"

Little red men

In the city, there are so many cars that walking without paying attention can be dangerous. We are lucky to have the little red man. With their bright red color, they warn us when the cars, motorcycles, and trucks are going by. We have to stay on the sidewalk until the little man changes his clothes to green.

The joy of music

Sometimes Grandfather takes me to listen to music. He knows that I behave and don't talk or fidget during the performance. The concerts are very long, but it's not just music. I look at each musician's face and see effort and concentration. I look at how the violin bows move up and down. I eagerly wait for a bang on the drums. And I laugh a little bit when the conductor moves. It's a good show!

A slow oven

"When are we going to eat dinner?" the youngest ones in the house ask. We're hungry, but the grown-ups say that good cooking takes time. "You should respect the cook for putting love and patience into everything he makes." They're right. The food was worth the waiting. Everything tastes great!

Patience in the fields

The bean we planted in class already has its first leaf. I had to wait days to see it, and I still cannot believe it. Some classmates thought that if they watered their plant more, it would grow quicker, but too much water isn't good for it. We learned that a good farmer must be patient to give the seeds the time they need to take hold in the soil and grow into strong plants.

Squirrel gatherers

The squirrels in the park have been gathering seeds from the ground for quite a while and taking them to their nest. They do it without complaining, day after day. That's how they get ready for when the cold weather comes. They are sure to have enough food stored for the winter.

Strawberries instead of cherries

I feel like eating cherries, but there aren't any in the store yet. "It's strawberry season now," the grocer explains to me. The produce man interrupts, "Each season has its fruits, and we have to learn to enjoy them when it is their time because that's when they are the most tasty."

Housetraining Spot

It takes time to learn, and it also takes time to teach. At home, we had to pick up lots of Spot's poop and clean up after his other accidents and mischief. We have to remind Spot to behave and to control himself until he gets outside. It takes a lot of patience to train Spot, but it is worth it.

Rainy day

It's raining, and all the children in class are looking sadly at the wet playground. "When will it stop so we can go out and play?" we ask our teacher over and over again. "Let's spend the time waiting for the rain to stop by doing something else that's fun," says the teacher. She brings us some games to play inside. There are always new things to learn indoors while we wait!

TEACHING THE VIRTUE OF PATIENCE

Children who practice the virtue of patience often share the following characteristics:

- Take joy in anticipation.
- Routinely delay immediate gratification.
- Accept difficulties and setbacks.
- Understand realistic timeframes.
- Refrain from cutting corners.
- Experience reduced impulsivity.
- Welcome challenges.

TEACHING BEING PATIENT WITH OTHERS

Help children practice the virtue of patience by cultivating the following practices when dealing with others:

- **Mindfulness** A concentrated focus on the present. Invite children to slow down and give their full attention to listening to a song or experiencing a work of art or a wonder of nature.

- **Generosity** Freely giving of one's time, care, and attention. Help children develop the skills necessary to patiently listen to the cares and concerns of others and avoid the inclination to try to solve the person's problem.

- **Tolerance** Joyfully recognizing that there are a diversity of opinions and perspectives in the world. Provide opportunities for children to learn about the diversity in the world and how they are part of it.

- **Empathy** Recognizing the humanity of others. Provide opportunities for children to walk in another's shoes so they can see things from that person's perspective.

- **Civility** Sincerely demonstrating respect and courtesy when speaking and interacting with others. Begin teaching this early in your child's life by practicing taking turns and modeling civil behavior as you go about your daily life.

TEACHING BEING PATIENT WITH ONESELF

It is only through patience that talent can develop. Growth and progress toward a goal is often incremental and not readily observable. Help children have an awareness that they might not get things right the first time or even the second or third time and that progress may be hard to see. Nevertheless, they need to be patient with their progress toward their goals. Not being patient with oneself can lead to unfulfilled potential or the premature abandonment of a dream. Practicing the virtue of patience increases the likelihood that children will achieve their goals and be happier with themselves.

TIPS FOR PARENTS

- Introduce games and activities that encourage problem solving and trial and error, such as construction toys, puzzles, and brainteasers.
- Wait patiently for traffic lights to change even when there are no cars in sight.
- Model waiting patiently in line and interacting with others when running errands.
- Plant and tend something indoors or outdoors and watch it grow over time.
- Take time to revel in the beauty of nature and in a job well done.
- Follow a relative's pregnancy or the growth of a younger sibling or cousin.
- Live in time with the seasons by enjoying seasonal fruits and vegetables, seasonal celebrations, and the weather.
- Read only one chapter of a well-loved novel per sitting or watch one episode of a favorite television series.
- Commemorate birthdays and anniversaries to mark the passage of time and highlight growth and change over time.
- Use family photos to point out progress or growth that can be seen.
- Keep a physical family calendar on which achievements and milestones can be recorded.
- Never forget that a virtue is transmitted by experiencing it.
- Let's practice patience.

CLASSROOM RESOURCES

Visit **www.LoyolaPress.com/Virtues** to access activities centered on social–emotional learning that supplement the messages from *The Virtue of Patience*.

LOYOLA PRESS.

3441 N. Ashland Avenue
Chicago, Illinois 60657
(800) 621-1008
www.loyolapress.com

THE VIRTUE OF PATIENCE

Text: **Aleix Cabrera and Vinyet Montaner**

Illustration: **Rosa M. Curto**

Design and layout: **Estudi Guasch, S.L.**

© **Gemser Publications, S.L. 2013**

El Castell, 38   08329 Teià (Barcelona, Spain)
www.mercedesros.com

Published in the United States in 2020 by Loyola Press.

ISBN: 978-0-8294-5038-5

Library of Congress Control Number: 2020930997

Printed in China.